The Fairytale Hairdresser

Picture Corgi

Abie Longstaff

Lauren Beard

Kittie Lacey was the best hairdresser in all the land.

People came from far, far away to have their hair washed and combed and cut and styled.

this book belongs to

....

Hair by Kittie

at Kittie's Cuts

THE FAIRYTALE HAIRDRESSER
A PICTURE CORGI BOOK 978 0 552 56186 0

First published in Great Britain as THE FAIRYTALE HAIRDRESSER by Red Fox, an imprint of Random House Children's Publishers UKA Random House Group Company Red Fox edition published 2011
This Picture Corgi edition published 2013

9 10 8

Picture Corgi Books are published by Random House Children's Publishers UK,
61–63 Uxbridge Road, London W5 5SA

www.randomhousechildrens.co.uk
www.randomhouse.co.uk

Addresses for companies within The Random House Group Limited can be found at:
www.randomhouse.co.uk/offices.htm THE RANDOM HOUSE GROUP Limited Reg. No. 954009
A CIP catalogue record for this book is available from the British Library.
Printed in China

Goldie x

Thanks, Kittie ♡ Red x

For K&E and for Gwen - A.L.

For my parents, John and June - L.B.

It was Kittie who brushed the
Fairy Godmother's long locks
till they sparkled and glittered.

She was the one who found the exact
shade of crimson to match Red Riding
Hood's cloak perfectly.

And if anyone ever needed a beard and sideburns trim, they knew just the place to go.

Sometimes Kittie had very difficult cases to deal with.

There were tall customers . . .

and tiny customers . . .

. . . and some very fussy ones!

"TOO HIGH!"

"Too curly!"

"TOO STRAIGHT!"

"too low!"

"Just right!"

She was often called out to visit
reclusive clients . . .

. . . in unusual places.

Indeed, Kittie was such a good hairdresser that she was
sure there was no hair she couldn't fix. Then one Saturday
she got her most difficult case of all.

Up in a high,

high tower

was a witch

with a very **big** problem.

Kittie gulped nervously
and rang the bell.

The door creaked open
and a golden river of hair flooded out!

"All this hair is taking over my tower!" screeched the Witch.
"I can't see a thing. It's affecting my work.
I can't make any evil potions and I'm sure
I've lost my glasses in there somewhere."

Kittie had never seen so much hair! It was all tangled and messy and frizzy, and some of the knots were the size of her fist. Was there even a person underneath all that?

Kittie took a deep breath and picked up her comb.

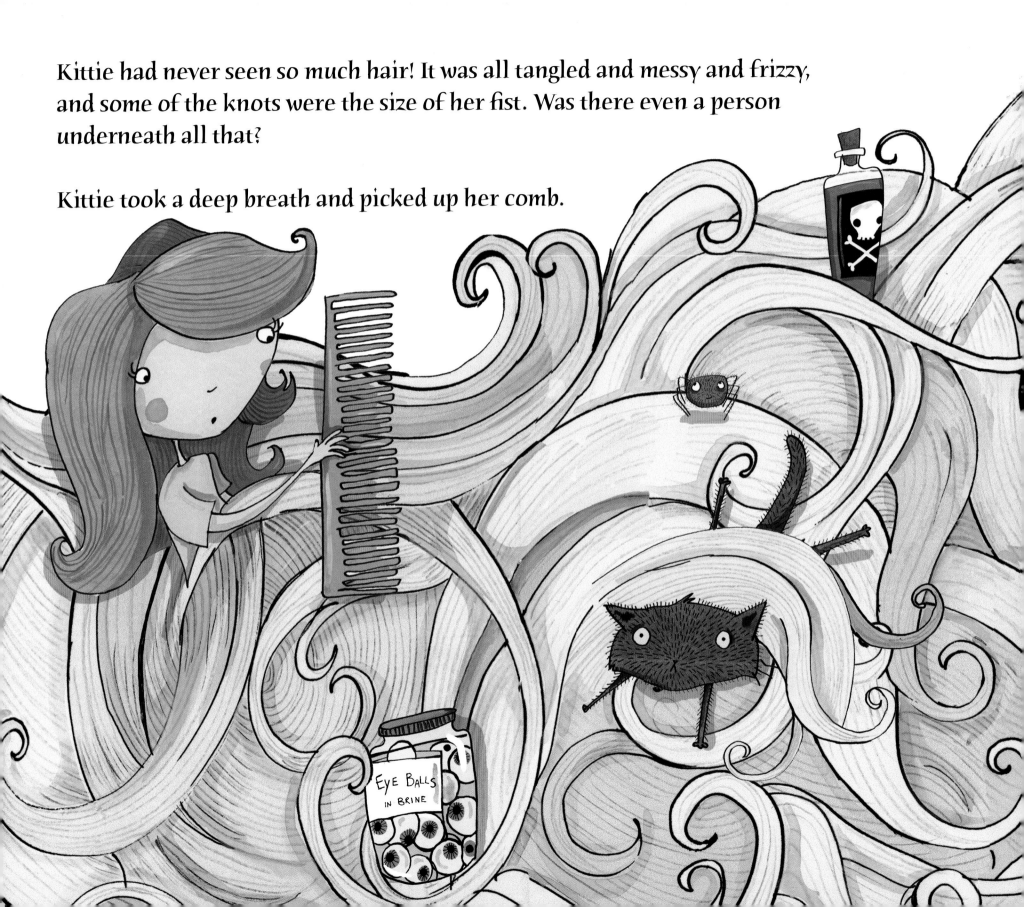

EYE BALLS IN BRINE

Bit-by-bit she parted the hair until . . .

at the centre she found a girl.

"I'm Rapunzel," said the girl. "Thank goodness you came!
I'm having a really bad hair day!"
Kittie smiled. "Don't worry, love! We'll have you looking gorgeous in no time!"

Kittie gathered the hair from all over the tower into a neat pile.
She sprayed every inch with conditioner.
Then she combed through the knots and trimmed the ends.

"Ah! That's much better!" cackled the Witch.
"Now I can get on with all my evil spells.

I need to make a poison apple

and a gingerbread house and a spindle.

But first . . . first I have to find a potion to make Kittie forget she was ever here."

After a whole day of hard work, Rapunzel's hair shimmered. It rippled down her back, across the tower floor, and curled into a beautiful pile in the corner.

Rapunzel loved her new hair. "It's so soft!" she said.

"But oh, Kittie! The Witch will never let you leave!"
"Don't worry," said Kittie. "I have a plan."

Kittie took three heavy bundles of hair
and began to plait. Then she winked
at Rapunzel and threw the long
plait out of the window.

Meanwhile, in the valley below, a handsome prince was riding by when he saw something very unusual lying on the grass.

The prince followed the plait all the way to the tower . . .

. . . and to his amazement, there he saw a beautiful girl leaning out
of the highest window. She had the longest, softest, silkiest
hair he had ever seen.

"Hello!" said Kittie, climbing down the plait.
"I'm Kittie and that is my friend Rapunzel."

"Oh, Rapunzel!" swooned the prince, gazing up at the window.

"Ohhh," sighed Rapunzel. (He really was a very handsome prince.)

Just then there was a terrible screech.
"Help!" cried Rapunzel. "The Witch is coming!"
"Jump, my love!" shouted the prince and he held out his arms.
Rapunzel jumped and fell all the way

down

down

down

down

down

into the arms of her prince.

The next day the Witch had a very different sort of visitor . . .

. . . and she soon found it was her turn to be locked away.

Of course Rapunzel and the prince were married.

It was the wedding event of the year! Everyone was there.

And guess who was invited to do the bride's hair?

Kittie Lacey, the best hairdresser in the land!

By Royal Appointment